24 Hour Telephone Renewals 020 8489 4560

HARINGEY LIBRARIES

THIS BOOK MUST BE RETURNED ON OR BEFORE
THE LAST DATE MARKED BELOW

To	ALEXANDRA PARK	
6 JUN 2017		
1 7 JUL 2017		
1 2 OCT 2017	1 9 MAY 2019	
1 8 NOV 2017	4 NOV 2019	
2 7 JAN 2018	2 JAN 2020	
2 5 APR 2018	6 FEB 2020	
1 1 JUN 2018		
2 1 AUG 2018	23 OCT 2020	
3 0 OCT 2018		

Online renewals – visit libraries.haringey.gov.uk

Published by Haringey Council's Communications Unit 1149.19 • 11/15

A... he
Cin... been
cr... John
C... ween
race... for an
ou... elling

R... up by
the... al Saint
Mar..., then as
a w... In 2013,
he... reating
them herself. She has since been nominated for The Sheffield
Children's Book Award 2015, and The Portsmouth Book Award
2016. Her published books include *How the Library (Not the Prince)
Saved Rapunzel* (written by Wendy Meddour), *Odd Socks* (written by
Michelle Robinson), *The Whopper* and the Bob and Flo series.

70001679068 9

This book is dedicated to all the glumps that want to be peebles
and all the peebles that want to be glumps.
W.M.

To Gerard
R.A.

Haringey Libraries	
AA	
Askews & Holts	20-Mar-2017
JF	
	3400018145

First published in Great Britain and in the USA in 2016 by
Frances Lincoln Children's Books
This first paperback edition published in Great Britain in 2017 by
Frances Lincoln Children's Books
74-77 White Lion Street, London N1 9PF
QuartoKnows.com
Visit our blogs at QuartoKnows.com

Text copyright © Wendy Meddour 2016
Illustrations copyright © Rebecca Ashdown 2016
The rights of Wendy Meddour and Rebecca Ashdown to be identified respectively as
the author and illustrator of this work have been asserted by them in accordance
with the Copyright, Designs and Patents Act, 1988 (United Kingdom).

All rights reserved

No part of this publication may be reproduced, stored in a retrieval system, or transmitted,
in any form, or by any means, electrical, mechanical, photocopying, recording or
otherwise without the prior written permission of the publisher or a licence
permitting restricted copying. In the United Kingdom such licences are
issued by the Copyright Licensing Agency, Barnard's Inn,
86 Fetter Lane, London, EC4A 1EN.

A catalogue record for this book is available from the British Library.

ISBN 978-1-84780-710-6

Illustrated digitally
Printed in China
1 3 5 7 9 8 6 4 2

The Glump and the Peeble

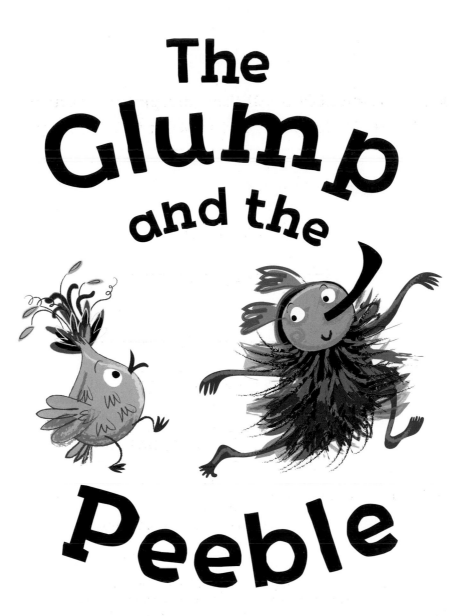

Written by
Wendy Meddour

Illustrated by
Rebecca Ashdown

Frances Lincoln
Children's Books

The Glump lived alone,
in a cave,
in a wood.
He tried to come out –
but he just never could.

He wanted to dance with the peebles at night.
He wanted to twirl in the glow of moonlight.
But glumps are not made for such dancing and fun –
in fact, what in the world has a glump ever done?

So he sat
all alone,
in a cave,
in a wood.
And tried to do nothing –
just like a glump should.

But then a small peeble skipped into the wood.
She was singing and dancing just like peebles should.

Then, NOT like a peeble –
she sighed and she frowned.

She stopped,

and she paused,

and she sat on the ground.

"I know that a peeble should dance every night.
I know I should twirl in the glow of moonlight.
But it makes me feel dizzy, I get hot and pink.

Why can't I sit still like a glump and just think?"

The Glump overheard, from his cave in the wood.
He tried to ignore her, just like a glump should.
But he couldn't.

He **coughed**.

Then he tried to sound brave:

"If you like, you can come
and sit still in my cave?"

The Peeble looked round at the glumpyish thing.
Then, blowing her nose on the tip of her wing,
she said, "I thought glumps were supposed to be **shy**!"

"We are. But we don't like to see peebles cry!
So **please** do come in and I'll clear you a space
to sit and just think in my quiet little place."

She followed the Glump and she closed her eyes tight.
Then she breathed in the still and the quiet of the night.

She thought about planets, she thought about stars.
She wondered if peebles could dance up on Mars?

She sat, without spinning,

not hot and not pink.

THE VERY FIRST PEEBLE TO SIT STILL AND THINK!

But when she had finished, the Glump looked quite down.
"Dear Glump," said the Peeble. "What's making you frown?"

"It's just that I wish I could dance in moonlight.
I'd love to have fun like a peeble at night.
But my feet are too big and I've got glumpy toes.
If I dance, I will trip and fall flat on my nose."

"Do you mean," said the Peeble,
"You don't like to sit,
thinking thoughts on your own
in the quietness of it?"
"No, I don't," said the Glump.
"I would rather be small,
and dainty and twirly.
NOT glumpy at all!"

The Peeble went quiet and she thought a bit more.
Then she said, as she got up and walked to the door,
"Come on, let me take you to twirl in the night."
"Oh, no!" said the Glump. "It just wouldn't feel right!"

"Try not to be nervous," the Peeble replied.
"You **cannot** be frightened of things you've not tried."

"All right," said the Glump,
"I will have a quick spin.
But please bring me home if I do not fit in!"

So they skipped through the woods
to a wide-open space,
where peebles were dancing all over the place!

"Just stretch out your arms wide and do what I do."

"It's no good," said the Glump. "I'm not peeble like you!"

"Come on," said the Peeble. "We're in the moonlight.

Just dance like a glump being peeble at night!"

So the Glump stretched his arms ...

then he twirled,

then he DANCED!

"Oh! I knew I'd be good if I just had the chance!"

The peebles all **cheered** to see such a sight.
A glump. Yes, a glump twirling under moonlight!
"It's a glump!" they all shouted. **"A glump!"** they all cried.
"He twirls like a peeble with arms stretched out wide!"

"Oh, Glump," said the Peeble. "I'm ever so proud!
I never knew peebles could CHEER quite this loud."

"And I," said the Glump, "am so glad you were brave,
and didn't mind coming to sit in my cave.
You're the FIRST EVER peeble to sit still and think!"
said the FIRST EVER glump that has danced until pink.

"Can we come back again? Can we dance in the night?"
"Yes, of course," beamed the Peeble. "You do it just right."

As they wandered together, back through the dark wood,
the Glump held the Peeble's hand, like a Glump should.
And he **skipped**, and he **twirled** – as she looked at the stars …
and wondered if peebles were dancing on Mars?

At last, in their cave, the Glump lay on the floor,
where he dreamt **peebly** dreams as he started to snore.

Whilst the Peeble curled up in her quiet little place –
and thought **glumpy** thoughts ...
with a smile on her face.

ALSO BY WENDY MEDDOUR AND REBECCA ASHDOWN,
PUBLISHED BY FRANCES LINCOLN CHILDREN'S BOOKS

How the Library (Not the Prince) Saved Rapunzel

978-1-84780-662-8

"Rapunzel, Rapunzel, please let down your hair,"
called the prince from down on the bottom stair.
He brought with him chocolates and roses red.
He wore leather trousers and shades on his head.

But Rapunzel doesn't think much of the prince. She sits in her tower block, silent and still –
until one day a very special letter arrives that gets Rapunzel on her feet at last…

"How refreshing to have a girl in a story whose fate lies within her own hands.
A brilliant picture book."
— *Malorie Blackman, Children's Laureate 2013–2015*

Frances Lincoln titles are available from all good bookshops.
You can also buy books and find out more about your favourite titles,
authors and illustrators on our website: www.franceslincoln.com